Daniel Tiger's Neighborhood

Naptime in the Neighborhood

Adapted by Alexandra Cassel Schwartz
Based on the screenplays by Monique D. Hall and Mary Jacobson
Poses and layouts by Jason Fruchter

Simon Spotlight
New York   London   Toronto   Sydney   New Delhi

SIMON SPOTLIGHT
An imprint of Simon & Schuster Children's Publishing Division
1230 Avenue of the Americas, New York, New York 10020
This Simon Spotlight paperback edition September 2020
© 2020 The Fred Rogers Company
All rights reserved, including the right of reproduction in whole or in part in any form.
SIMON SPOTLIGHT and colophon are registered trademarks of Simon & Schuster, Inc.
For information about special discounts for bulk purchases, please contact Simon & Schuster
Special Sales at 1-866-506-1949 or business@simonandschuster.com.
Manufactured in the United States of America 0720 LAK
10 9 8 7 6 5 4 3 2 1
ISBN 978-1-5344-6903-7 (pbk)
ISBN 978-1-5344-6904-4 (eBook)

It was a beautiful day in the neighborhood, and Daniel was at school.

"Hi, neighbor!" said Daniel. "I'm playing trains with Miss Elaina. Choo, choo!"

"All aboard!" said Miss Elaina.

Conductor Daniel and Miss Elaina were having so much fun playing at school.

Teacher Harriet told the class they had a few more minutes to play before naptime.

Daniel and Miss Elaina made a train track for their train. They even added some little bugs as their train passengers.

"Bugga, bugga, choo, choo!" Miss Elaina said.

They both giggled at their bug train.

Before they could finish their train track, Teacher Harriet strummed her guitar for naptime. She sang,

"It's time for a rest. It's time to settle down. Pack up your toys, get quiet all around."

Daniel and Miss Elaina didn't want to stop playing.
"What about our train?" Daniel asked, worried.
"I know it's hard to stop playing, but it's naptime now. Your train will be right here for you to finish after naptime," Teacher Harriet said.

Daniel and his friends put their toys down and found their nap mats.

Everyone got on their mat to take a rest, but Daniel wasn't feeling sleepy. He wanted to talk to Miss Elaina about their bug train.

"Bugga, bugga, choo, choo!" Daniel said.

He and Miss Elaina giggled loudly. Teacher Harriet came over to check on them.

"You don't need to go to sleep if you're not tired," she said, "but you do need to rest quietly without talking so you don't wake your friends." Teacher Harriet sang,

"Close your eyes, snuggle, or take a deep breath. . . .
You can do what helps you rest."

Miss Elaina snuggled her stuffie and then closed her eyes. She was ready to rest.

Daniel wondered what he could do to help him rest. He remembered he sometimes closes his eyes and uses his imagination, and that helps him rest.

Daniel made believe he was on a sleepy train! He sang to himself,

♪ *"Choo, choo! The quiet-time train is chugging along, singing its quiet-time song. The stars are twinkling in the sky as the quiet-time train sings a sweet lullaby. Everyone's drifting off to sleep, dreaming sweet dreams without a peep, as the quiet-time train sings a sweet lullaby!"* ♪

When Daniel opened his eyes, naptime wasn't over. He was still having trouble resting, so he sang quietly,

"Close your eyes, snuggle, or take a deep breath. . . . You can do what helps you rest."

That gave him another idea.
"Teacher Harriet?" Daniel whispered. "Can I rest with a book?"
Teacher Harriet liked that idea. She gave Daniel a book to read to help him rest.

Daniel felt calm while he rested quietly with his book.
"Meow, meow," Katerina said loudly. Now she was having trouble resting.

"Reading a book helped me rest," Daniel said to Katerina. Daniel sang,

♪ ♪ *"Close your eyes, snuggle, or take a deep breath. . . .* ♪
You can do what helps you rest." ♪

Katerina tried closing her eyes, snuggling her baby doll, and taking a big, deep breath. Then she felt better and could rest. The classroom was nice and quiet for naptime.

When naptime was over, Teacher Harriet sang,

"Wake up your eyes, wake up your nose.
Wiggle your fingers, wiggle your toes.
Stretch and shake yourself awake!"

Everyone stretched and then put their nap mats away. It was time to play!

Daniel and Miss Elaina went back to their train. It was right where they left it—just like Teacher Harriet said!

Daniel and Miss Elaina had more energy after naptime.
They finished their train track and took their bugs for a ride.
"Bugga, bugga, choo, choo!" they called.

After a lot of playing and learning at school, it was time to go home. Daniel's mom came to pick him up with his baby sister, Margaret.

"Hi, Mom! Hi, Margaret!" Daniel said.

Margaret yawned loudly. It was time for her nap.

Conductor Daniel was ready to help.
"All aboard the naptime train!" Daniel said. "Choo, choo! Next stop: home for naptime!"

Margaret started to cry when they got home.

"Why is she sad?" Daniel asked his mom.

"She is just tired. She will feel better after she rests," Mom Tiger said.

Mom Tiger put Margaret in her crib and turned the lights off in her room.

Margaret was still a little fussy in her crib, so Daniel and Mom Tiger sang,

♪ ♪ *"Close your eyes, snuggle, or take a deep breath. . . .* ♪
You can do what helps you rest." ♪

Then Daniel found something special for Margaret to snuggle.
"Here's your Pandy," he whispered.
Margaret snuggled with her Pandy and fell asleep.

"I found what helps me rest at school, and then I helped Margaret rest at home," Daniel said. "What helps YOU rest? Ugga Mugga!"